CW01512018

THE UNEXPURGATED ADVENTURES OF

SHERLOCK HOLMES

BOOK 4

MY FIRST PROPER RURAL MURDER

by NP Sercombe

The un-edited manuscript originally entitled
The Boscombe Valley Mystery written by
Dr. John Watson and Sir Arthur Conan Doyle

Illustrations by Emily Snape

Published by EVA BOOKS 2019 – c/o Harry King Films Limited
        1&2 The Barn
        West Stoke Road
        Lavant
        n/r Chichester
        West Sussex PO18 9AA

A CIP catalogue record for this book is available from the British Library.

ISBN 978-1-9996961-3-9 (Hardback)

Book layout & Cover design by Clare Brayshaw.

Cover illustration by Emily Snape.

Set in Bruce Old Style.

Prepared and printed by: York Publishing Services Ltd
64 Hallfield Road, Layerthorpe, York YO31 7ZQ

Tel: 01904 431213

Website: www.yps-publishing.co.uk

THE UNEXPURGATED ADVENTURES OF

SHERLOCK HOLMES

Books in the Series:

Nicholas Sercombe is a writer and producer for film and television. He has been lucky enough to work in comedy for most of the Holocene period with some of the greatest performers and writers. He is most comfortable when reading Conan Doyle and even happier when re-writing these extraordinarily entertaining stories by Dr. John Watson.

Emily Snape is a coffee addicted, London based illustrator, who's work can be found internationally in books, magazines, on the web, television and even buses.

She studied at Central Saint Martins, Bristol and Kingston and is rarely found without a pencil in her hand. She loves sketching in the streets of London and thinks life is too short for matching socks.

For lovers of the deerstalker hat who enjoy laughing

My First Proper Rural Murder

(published in The Strand in October 1891 as
THE BOSCOMBE VALLEY MYSTERY *by*
Dr. Watson and Arthur Conan Doyle)

We were seated at breakfast one morning at 221B Baker Street. Mrs. Hudson had brought in a telegram. It was from Sherlock Holmes, and ran in this way:

"My dear fellow, have you a couple of days to spare? Have just been wired for from the West of England in connection with Boscombe Valley tragedy. Shall be glad if you will come with me. Air and scenery are perfect. We leave Paddington by the 11.15."

'Mrs. Hudson,' I said, 'perhaps you would be good enough to pass me that pen and paper from the bureau over there, so I may write a reply.'

'Certainly not, Doctor!' said Mrs. Hudson. 'This situation has got to stop. Instead of sending another telegram in reply, why don't you just tell him, to his face?'

The situation to which our housekeeper was referring was the quarantine of silence that Holmes and I had placed one another into. After we had solved the previous, sordid mystery, *The Case of the Randy Stepfather,* about how Miss Mary Sutherland had been jilted at the altar by her perverted stepfather posing as a Jewish bridegroom, Holmes's beautiful sister, Rachel, had taken a shine to me at a family celebration and called on me the next day in Baker Street. We had dined out, never to return to the apartment that night. Holmes was very protective of his only sister and assumed that Rachel had stayed with me at my house in Queensbury Place, South Kensington, where I kept my medical practice, and had been rogered bandy by yours truly. Consequently, Holmes had put me into Coventry.

However, he was wrong. Our evening was purely romantic; one of joyful and innocent flirtation over a fine supper at Rules. When it came to the moment of truth, Rachel took off in a hansom to her room at The Goring, the little tease! I ended up camping out at the practice because my bedroom at Baker Street was beyond practical and sanitary use, thanks to the great detective defiling my bed with the substantial Miss Mary Sutherland for an afternoon of carnal *amour*. Tit-for-tat, I had put him into Coventry as well. Therefore, for nearly a week now, we communicated only by telegram.

'Mrs. Hudson!' cried Holmes tetchily, snatching a look at his pocket watch. 'Don't just stand there! The good Doctor would like to write a telegram note, no doubt addressed to me, that will be an answer to my invitation. Our new client will not wait.' Holmes held up a handwritten letter. 'Kindly help him do it.'

'No, Mr. Holmes, I shall not! This quarrel has lasted too long. Where has the lively conversation gone to? Where is the laughter seeping through the floorboards down into my kitchen?' She walked up to our breakfast table and jabbed her forefinger at both of us. 'I demand that you put an end to this feud. RIGHT NOW!'

'I would resolve it immediately, within a flash,' I protested, and then pointed at Holmes, 'but he won't let me in.' I tapped my temple with my finger, confirming my opinion of a mental impasse.

In response, Holmes sat back in his chair, rested his elbows on each arm, pursed his lips in a sneer and flicked his long white fingers in dismissive fashion.

'Then we shall have to nip his Achilles heel, won't we?' whispered Mrs. Hudson, in hushed tones but with serious intent, which surprised me. Then, for the first time since I had made her acquaintance, I watched the soft, sensitive and generous Mrs. Hudson boil herself up into a fiery temper. She used a deep intake of breath to build up her body to its full height, which caused her face to redden and her cheeks to ripen, like Kentish coxes. Then, she held on, for a long time, in sufferance. She had caught our full attention, and she had done so quite successfully because we goggled in amazement. When we thought that she was about to burst, she suddenly sprang forwards and snatched the letter from Holmes's left hand. She folded it up and placed it down the front of her blouse. Holmes's jaw dropped as far as his face would allow.

'There! Now that I have your attention, Mr. Holmes, we shall stay here and discuss this matter until you are friends once again.'

I could see that Holmes was amazed by her belligerent determination. Just to add pressure, I changed my position to mimic his own pose. I was now locked in position opposite him. I stared at him, eye-to-eye, until his face betrayed annoyance and intolerance, his eye muscles twitching involuntarily, and he kept stabbing a glance at Mrs. Hudson but not wishing to say anything. After what seemed like a minute, but was probably two or more, he threw himself backwards in a violent movement, sprang up from his chair, threw his napkin down onto his seat and looked at both of us.

'Watson! If we are to answer the call for my help dutifully, we must pack at once. We have only half an hour.'

He marched off through the room to his bedroom, leaving Mrs. Hudson and I to smile at each other with satisfaction. I was thrilled to be out of Coventry. I stood up and accepted Holmes's letter now offered to me by Mrs. Hudson. I took a glimpse at the neat handwriting, made in violet ink, and put it to my nose. The paper smelled of a fine perfume, and it wasn't Mrs. Hudson's. This, I deduced, was the letter from the bureau of a wealthy lady.

I looked at Mrs. Hudson as I pocketed the letter. She was a lady too, but a clever one – she had placed jeopardy against the single, supreme priority in Sherlock's life, which is to engage his massive brain in solving new cases. And, as I suspected, from adventures gone by, he needed me, to be used as his sounding-board and to help him fathom these mysteries.

'Would you like me to give you a hand with your packing, John?' she whispered, whilst making a rather suggestive movement of her tongue to moisten her lips.

'Surely we do not have enough time?' I whispered back. 'For any of...' I made the same tongue movement in return, '...that?'

She wore a languid smile, a naughty one that I recognised only too well, and she wasn't putting on because her favourite boys were friends again. I detected the familiar, heady atmosphere of impending intimacy.

She moved in close to me. I could feel her breath on my neck, my follicles tingling. Without further ado, she skipped out of the room and through to my bedroom, her finger beckoning me in. What we achieved in the little time available to us, in just a few minutes, is still a mystery to me, but the proof was in the pudding. A few minutes later, there I was, standing on the landing, ready to depart, with my case packed and my constitution consummated, Mrs. Hudson wielding the ostrich feather duster, when Holmes marched out of his bedroom. He was surprised to be the last on parade. He stopped in his tracks and flicked his eyes between Mrs. Hudson and me, our very innocent activities regarded suspiciously. Then, the prospect of this new case out in the shires over-excited him; his face lit up, he strode over to the rack, whisked a herringbone coat off its hook, pinched the top of a new-style hat – a cloth one that was unfamiliar to me – and flicked up his curly-wurly cane in a flourish, and turned to face us.

'The game's a-foot!' he cried, and we dashed down the stairs and into a hansom.

* * *

We were in the cab with our valises, rattling away on the cobbles towards Paddington Station. I handed him the client's letter that had been hijacked by Mrs. Hudson. He waved it aside nonchalantly.

'Keep it, Doctor. I memorised it, word for word.' Ah! Now here was a thought: Mrs. Hudson had had the right idea, and it had worked perfectly, but Holmes had not needed to accede to the blackmail. I smiled to myself, because the only possible reason he could have wanted to reach a compromise on the Coventry was

When it came to packing, Mrs Hudson knew all the tricks.

that he knew the value, maybe even the necessity, of including me on this new adventure. But then my face darkened when I remembered how I was always the financier of our previous adventures. Maybe he needed me for my money more than my glowing geniality...

'Is there any money in this, Holmes?' I enquired. Naturally, I knew that it was a rhetorical question, and, as usual, there was no answer. Instead, Holmes gazed out of the window. I had no doubt that he was deep in thought, as we rattled through the London streets. After a minute or so, I held up the letter again. 'Perhaps I should read it, Holmes, to give me some background to this new mystery?'

'That will not be possible in the brief moment we have before departure. I shall relate the relevant details to you once we are installed in the carriage and we have commenced our journey.'

I looked at my pocket watch. Indeed, he was correct, so I folded the letter into my breast pocket. Two minutes later, we were striding down the platform, with Holmes leading the way, his tall, gaunt figure made even gaunter by his long grey travelling cloak and a new style of hat.

'Holmes,' I hailed. 'What of this new cloth cap you are wearing? I have never seen you wear one like it before.'

He turned to look at me over his shoulder. 'It is a deerstalker. It is worn when hunting deer.'

'How exciting, Holmes. I have never stalked deer.'

'We shall be stalking Inspector Lestrade, of Scotland Yard! A quarry that is much easier to bring to heel than the wily and cunning deer. Lestrade is the buffoon who has been placed in charge of clearing up this mystery.

You may remember him in connection with the *Study in Scarlet*.'

'I remember him, but I don't follow you, Holmes. Why would you dress yourself in a close-fitting cloth cap to approach the idiotic plod?'

'Because of this...' Sherlock Holmes stopped in his tracks. I stood still and watched in wonder as he removed the cap, untied the corded bow on the top, which released a cloth flap either side, donned the cap again and tugged it down tight. With great alacrity he fastened the flaps under his chin, thus hiding his ears completely, and then beamed a silly smiley face at me, his hands outstretched.

'Now, Doctor, I will not be able to hear a word that the buffoon says! None of his inane ramblings or theories or hopeless deductions!'

I clapped my hands together and laughed out loud. 'Bravo, Holmes! Bravo!'

We resumed our walk down the platform. 'I thought you might like that,' he said, as I drew up alongside him. 'I say, Holmes, why don't we call this ear-flapping cap "The Lestrade?"'

'Ha! Excellent, Watson! We shall do just that. Do you know, I am pleased that you have come along. It is really very good of you. It makes a considerable difference to me, having someone with me on whom I can thoroughly rely.'

I was chuffed! 'Surely, Holmes, I am your *only* reliable person?'

Holmes stumbled for a moment, but then regained his balance. 'Of course, you are, Watson,' he chirruped. Goodness me, he was in a good mood! 'I can think of nobody more suitable. If, for instance, I was to enlist local aid, to wherever I was going to, it would either be worthless or biased.'

'Nor would anybody else understand the way in which we work. You, analysing the data and making the deduction. Me, listening to you, reasoning with you and, occasionally, shooting people for you.'

'I have said it already -- you are invaluable, Watson. Now, would you be so kind as to keep those two corner seats in the second carriage there whilst I go and buy the tickets.'

Buy the tickets?! Well, I nearly fainted! I missed a step, tripped, corrected myself and drew to a halt, feeling very queer. By then the great detective had already taken a route directly towards the ticket office.

'Holmes -- are you absolutely sure about that?' I murmured to myself, stupidly out loud. He stopped, turned around to face me, smiled from ear to ear and then lifted his finger in a Eureka moment.

'You are perfectly correct, Watson. It slipped my mind that you handle the finances. This recent impasse between us must have upset me more than I thought. My dear chap, I do hope that you are not offended. I shall reserve the seats instead.'

I watched as Holmes changed direction and sauntered towards the waiting train. Dammit! Me and my big mouth! I checked for my wallet and set a new course for the ticket office.

* * *

We were in a public carriage but had a corner to ourselves, away from the general public, but surrounded by the immense pile of papers that Holmes had brought with him. Among these he rummaged and read, with intervals of notetaking and meditation, until we were past Reading. Each item was screwed up into a ball and discarded upon the floor. Eventually, he looked down and he was surrounded by a mountain range of litter.

'Have you heard anything of the case?' he asked.

'No, not a word. You bid me not to read the letter here.' I patted my breast pocket.

'Indeed. I have just been looking through all the recent papers in order to master the particulars. Unfortunately, the London press has not had very full accounts. It seems, from what I gather, to be one of those simple cases which are so extremely difficult.'

'Holmes, that sounds like complete gobbledegook.'

'That sounds a little paradoxical, Watson, but it is profoundly true. Singularity is almost invariably a clue. The more featureless and commonplace a crime is, the more difficult it is to bring it home. In this case, however, they have established a very serious case against the son of the murdered man.'

'It is a murder then?'

'Well, it is conjectured to be so. I shall take nothing for granted until I have the opportunity of looking personally into it. I will explain the state of things to you, as far as I have been able to understand it, in a very few words.'

'Not before you clear that mess up, d'you hear?' said a voice from behind me. I swung round to see the conductor looking on imperiously. He was a young man of medium build, with a kindly face that sent out signals of authority but under the duress of the job in hand. 'Littering on Great Western Railways is an offence!'

'I think you will find that it is not litter, my dear fellow,' said Holmes. 'Kindly move on and leave us alone so that I may relate information of the utmost importance to my colleague here.'

'Clear it up, or I shall report you to the police.'

'Your name, dear sir?'

'Conductor Adler.'

'You are Peter Adler.' The fellow's jaw dropped down like a trapdoor.

'I am!' he admitted. 'But how did you know?'

'I thought so!' snapped Holmes. 'And the name of your favourite uncle is?'

'Frederick?'

Officer Adler glanced at me quizzically. I shrugged my shoulders. We both returned our gaze to the great detective.

'Peter,' said Holmes, very quietly, 'you may be the eldest boy of four but that doesn't give you the right to tell me, a member of the public, me in particular, what to do with my chattels.'

'I *am* the eldest!' he ejaculated, with astonishment written all over his face. 'And how did you know that I have three brothers, all younger than me?'

'It is my business to know, Peter. Let me give you a clue. This pile of paper may look like litter to you, but I can assure you, it is essential reading matter when connected to a master detective.'

His eyes widened. 'You are a master detective, sir?'

'That I am. And this is my assistant, Dr. Watson.'

'Watson?! You are the detectives in that magazine, *The Strand*? YOU are Sherlock Holmes?'

The great detective inclined his head in the affirmative. All of a sudden, Peter Adler jumped forwards, his face the very epitome of gleeful happiness, with his hand outstretched. He pumped Holmes's mitt and then my own.

'Marvellous! Bloody marvellous!' he enthused at me. 'I read all of your adventures, Doctor, every issue. You write so bloomin' well, I'm on the edge of my seat every week, I am!'

'Thank you, Peter, for those kind words. I am afraid that the editor is a bit of a butcher, but I suppose that he leaves us with the essence of each mystery, hopefully enough?'

'I'll say it again, Doctor... Bloody marvellous! I'm always trying to work out what's happened from the beginning, and that's the trick, you see? Trying to work out what's happened before you get there, if you know what I mean...Now, what are you two famous persons doing down here *slumming it* in second class, eh?'

'The good Doctor here was too mean to buy us first class tickets.'

'Ha! I am sure the Doctor made a mistake. It won't do, dear sirs. Now! You gents follow me...'

The next thing we knew, we were in our own, first-class compartment, with the compliments of South Western Railways via its enthusiastic representative, Peter Adler. Moreover, after he had placed us in this position, he went back to retrieve the papers that Holmes had left on the floor. He rolled them all into a gigantic ball and tossed them up on the rack. Then, he left us, to find, he said, some complimentary refreshments. Now, we had the carriage to ourselves.

'How did you know that his name is Peter?'

'He has monogrammed cuff links. A "p" and an "a." It was a calculated guess that Peter was the likely name.'

'Fair enough. But how did you know that he was the eldest child?'

'You should visit the London archive and read a census or two, Doctor. There, you will find, that Peter is the first given name to the inherited surname of Adler, per generation.'

'And the deduction that he had three brothers?'

'The fourth son is named after the father's eldest brother. The fact that his uncle's first name tripped off the tongue so easily, led me to believe that he was probably the eldest. If you were to study genealogy, Watson, this would have been obvious.'

'Yes, I can see that now, Holmes. But how did you know there were four in the first place?'

The door to the compartment was opened by Peter Adler, just as Holmes gave me his deduction. He was carrying a tray of sandwiches and Indian pale ale, which he placed on the table.

'Take note of this man's nose. It is a Huguenot nose, unless I am mistaken? Mr. Adler here is of French descent.'

Peter Adler stroked his nose and nodded his head a little.

'*Ipso facto*, he is a Protestant and therefore unlikely to be in a family larger than six persons, as opposed to one of Catholic origins which would have yielded a much larger crop. Therefore, it was a reasonable estimate of four children only.'

'Remarkable!' uttered our fanatical conductor, shaking his head in wonder as he left us and closed the compartment door.

'I say, Holmes,' I wondered. 'Is he any relation to Irene Adler?'*

'Don't be ridiculous, Watson!'

Suitably informed and rebuked, I sat back into my seat and gazed out of the window at the bland countryside flashing by. My mind wandered between admiration for the great detective's depth of knowledge outside the humdrum of everyday life, and what his sister, Rachel, might look like in a position of extreme intimacy. This caused a stirring of my trouser bone. The great detective glanced over. I became embarrassed. I had to cross my legs hastily to try and disguise my lurid thoughts, and so I resorted to a distraction.

'So, my dear Holmes, what awaits us at the end of this line?'

'A good question, Watson, and the answer to which might stop you thinking about my sister.'

I crossed my legs over the other way.

'That's better. Boscombe Valley is a country district not very far from Ross-on-Wye, in Herefordshire. The largest landed proprietor in that part is a Mr. Gerald Turner, who made his money in Australia, and returned some years ago to the old country. One of the farms which he held, that of Hatherley, was let to Mr. Peter McCartney, who was also an ex-Australian. The men had known each other in the Colonies, so that it was not unnatural that when they came to settle down, they should do so as near to each other as possible. Turner

---

*   see *A Balls-Up in Bohemia*

*My affection for the great detective's sister in my fantasies
was a very sensitive subject!*

was apparently the richer man, so McCartney became his tenant, but still remained, it seems, upon terms of perfect equality, as they were frequently together. McCartney had one son, a lad of eighteen, and Turner had an only daughter of the same age, but neither of them had wives living.'

I found this highly suspicious. What were the chances of each friend losing his wife? I told Holmes so, but he batted it away as a complete irrelevance.

'Tsk! Pray, may I continue?' I nodded. 'Well, it seems that these two men avoided the society of the neighbouring English families, and to have led retired lives, though both the McCartneys were fond of sport, and were frequently seen at the race meetings of the area. McCartney kept two servants – a man and a girl. Turner had a considerable household, some half dozen at the least. That is as much as I have been able to gather about the families. Now for the facts.

'On June 3rd – that is, on Monday last – McCartney left his house at Hatherley about three in the afternoon and walked down to the Boscombe Pool, which is a small lake, formed by the spreading out of the stream, which runs down by the Boscombe Valley. He had been out with his serving-man in the morning at Ross, and he had told the man that he must hurry, as he had an appointment of importance to keep at three. From that appointment he never came back alive.

'From Hatherley Farmhouse to the Boscombe Pool is a quarter of a mile, and two people saw him as he passed over this ground. One was an old woman, whose name is not mentioned, and the other was William Crowder, a gamekeeper in the employ of Mr. Turner. Both these witnesses depose that Mr. McCartney was walking alone. The gamekeeper adds that within a few minutes of his seeing Mr. McCartney pass, he had seen his son, Mr. James McCartney, going the same way with a gun under his arm. To the best of his belief, the father was actually in sight at the time, and the son was following him. He thought no more of the matter until he heard in the evening of the tragedy that had occurred.

'The two McCartneys were seen after the time when William Crowder, the gamekeeper, lost sight of them. The Boscombe Pool is thickly wooded around, with just a fringe of grass and reeds round the edge. A girl of fourteen, Patience Morahan, who is the daughter of the lodge-keeper of the Boscombe Valley estate, was in one of the woods picking flowers. She states that while she was there, she saw, at the border of the wood and close by the lake, Mr. McCartney and his son, and that they appeared to be having a violent quarrel.'

'Well, we know how easy that can happen, don't we Holmes?'

'Don't interrupt, Watson! Anyway, the girl says she heard Mr. McCartney the elder using very strong language to his son, and she saw the latter raise up his hand as if to strike his father. She was so frightened by their violence that she ran away. When she reached home, she told her mother that she had left the two McCartneys quarrelling near Boscombe Pool, and that she was afraid that they were going to fight. She had hardly said the words when young Mr. McCartney came running up to the lodge to say that he had found his father dead in the wood, and to ask for the help of the lodge-keeper. He was much excited, without either his gun or his hat, and his right hand and sleeve were observed to be stained with fresh blood. On following him they found the dead body of his father stretched out upon the grass beside the Pool. The head had been beaten in by a blow of some heavy and blunt weapon. The injuries were such as might very well have been inflicted by the butt-end of his son's gun, which was found lying on the grass within a few paces of the body. Under these circumstances the young man was instantly arrested, and a verdict of "Willful Murder" having been returned at the inquest on Tuesday, he was on Wednesday brought before the magistrates at Ross, who have referred the case to the next Assizes. Those are the main facts of the case as they came out before the Coroner and at the police court.'

'I could hardly imagine a more damning case,' I remarked. 'If ever circumstantial evidence pointed to a criminal it does so here.'

'Circumstantial evidence is a very tricky thing,' answered Holmes thoughtfully; 'it may seem to point very straight to one thing, but if you shift your own point of view a little, you may find it pointing in an equally uncompromising manner to something entirely different. It must be confessed, however, that the case looks exceedingly grave against the young man, and it is very possible that he is indeed the culprit. There are several people in the neighbourhood, however, and among them, Miss Turner, the daughter of the neighbouring landowner, who believe in his innocence, and who have retained Lestrade to work out the case in his interest. Lestrade, being rather puzzled, has referred the case to me, and hence it is that two middle-aged gentlemen are flying westward at fifty miles an hour, instead of quietly digesting their breakfasts at home.'

'I am afraid,' said I, 'if I was one of the magistrates,

I'd take Mr. McCartney outside and hang him from the nearest tree.'

'So sayeth the disciple of Hippocrates, the preserver of human life!'

A moment of silent irony settled over the two of us. Then, we broke into laughter. This was the true icebreaker, the moment of realisation that our friendship had been healed completely.

'He may be guilty,' said Holmes, 'but there is nothing more deceptive than an obvious fact.'

'There are plenty of them!' I added. 'The facts are so obvious that you will find little credit to be gained out of this case. This may be a wasted journey.'

'Don't be too hasty, Doctor. We may chance to hit upon some other obvious facts which may have been by no means obvious to Mr. Lestrade. You know me too well to think that I am boasting when I say that I shall either confirm or destroy his theory by means which he is quite incapable of employing, or even of understanding. To take the first example to hand, I know very well that in your bedroom the window is upon the right-hand side, and yet I question whether Mr. Lestrade would have noted even so self-evident a thing as that by the way in which you shave your face.'

At the mention of my bedroom I sat bolt upright and screwed my face up. I was shocked by Holmes bringing up the subject so soon after the resolution of our argument. He read my thoughts.

'Calm down, Watson! Let me tell you that I have a confession to make about your bedroom, in the respect that I let you believe your own supposition that Miss Mary Sutherland and I had indulged ourselves lustfully at the expense of your bedroom. In fact, nothing untoward happened between the two of us. I could have told you on that day, a week ago, but I thought it would be more amusing at the time to let you make up your own mind about what had happened. You thought the worst.'

'But you made the same, incorrect deduction about Rachel and I!' I protested. 'And we never spent the night together anyway.'

'I was not incorrect in my deduction. I know that Rachel stayed at The Goring. I was being spiteful about your incorrect supposition, which is why I didn't tell you. I apologise, my dear Watson.'

I laughed out loud, more or less as a relief, to know that Holmes had taken advantage of my good nature. 'Your apology is heartily accepted, my friend! I cannot believe that we played each other out to such an extent that we strained our friendship so.' I leaned forward towards him. 'But what on Earth happened in my bedroom that afternoon?'

'Ha! Well, I took her to the room, which was all neat and tidy, as Mrs. Hudson had left it that morning. I positioned the Mummy Couch next to the adjoining wall so that she would be comfortable when earwigging our impending conversation with her scurrilous stepfather. She was standing very close to me, and I could hear her breathing getting heavy, but I put it down to the warm weather. Just as I turned away from her – I was searching for an empty glass to act as an amplifier for the adjoining wall and listen to the upcoming interview – she made her move on me. Suddenly, a strong hand grasped my posterior. Before I could take control of the situation, she was using both of her hands to knead my buttocks.'

My eyes shot out, like organ stops! 'Oh my God, Holmes! She is a very powerful woman!'

'I was pulled backwards and flipped around onto her bosom, and into her waiting arms. Her lips pressed down onto my face. She was hot, in a fever, perspiring. She was much too strong for me.'

'Gosh, Holmes *that* strong!'

'Yes. In my distress, I remembered reading about grizzly bears, and what to do if confronted and cornered by one in the wild, such account written by G. Scofield, a man of the British Columbian mountains. His recommendation was to lie supine, pretend to be dead, and the beast will lose interest.'

'Or eat you!' We laughed. What a joy it was to be back in humorous harmony again. 'And what happened?'

Holmes leaned in much closer to me and lowered his voice. 'Well, here's the fascinatingly unique part of the story. I feigned a faint. I went limp in her embrace, like a faking grass snake. Many moments passed, and I wondered what was happening because I had my eyes tight shut, not even sneaking a peek. Eventually, I felt the tautness in her muscles relax. She picked me up, entirely, and, very tenderly, placed me upon your bed. She stroked my face, and then my body, as gently as if I was a sleeping child.' The great detective paused to catch his breath. 'But then, she broadened the horizons of her tenderness.'

'Uh-oh!'

'Her hands moved south and broke into the engine room. She rummaged around and found what she was so desperately looking for, and she was triumphant.'

'My goodness Holmes, what did you...it...do?'

'As you know, dear Doctor, I am an accomplished actor. I think that I played my part with dedication.'

'Quite! But Holmes, as a doctor, and knowing you as a friend, and how your constitution is, I am amazed that you were able to suppress your natural instincts in a situation of such intimate stimulation.'

'Oh, I haven't finished yet! When her manual endeavours failed, she tried another technique.'

Holmes stared at me, deadly serious, and then he stuck his tongue out until it touched his nose; it was one of his party tricks. The penny dropped.

'She plumbed your plums? You lucky chap! And you hadn't even taken her out to dinner!'

'Well, now, you are perfectly correct, up to a point, Watson. You see, once she had tested me to the next limit – and *still* she didn't get a reaction...'

I clapped my hands in appreciation. 'Bravo, Holmes! Encore!'

'...SHE WENT BERSERK!' The detective threw his arms up in despair. 'First, she beat her chest. Then, she ran around the room, clearing tabletops and shelves with her burly arms. She jumped up and down. She gave tongue to the gods!'

'At least she found some sort of use for her tongue!'

'She ululated like a banshee! Then, she jumped up onto your bed, tossed all the blankets off and ripped the linen to shreds with her bare teeth!'

I collapsed into laughter and slapped my sides. This was the funniest thing! I had a vision of this huge, powerful woman running amok at 221B, like a whirling dervish, with Holmes wriggling around at her feet trying to avoid being stamped to death! Holmes started to laugh too. 'Now you know why your room was so disrupted!' he ejected, in between bellows.

Just then, Peter Adler interrupted us with a knock on the compartment door. Through the glass, we could see that his uniform was now splattered with soot. He was accompanied by a small, round man, with a vacant look, dressed in a boiler suit and wearing a cap, and covered from head to toe in soot. I applied some of my friend's methods, looked the fellow up and down, and deduced he must be the engine driver.

Holmes jammed his boot against the door – he was determined to finish off his story before letting them in. He leaned forwards to me delivered the conclusion in a truncated whisper. 'Anyway, her foul temper gave her temporary blindness. I slid onto the floor and escaped on all fours. The next time we saw her, she had turned into Madame Whiplash.'

'My goodness me, Holmes, you must have been scampering across the floor, like a spider!' I spluttered, still creased up. 'What a story!'

Holmes lifted his boot. Peter Adler opened the door. Holmes sat up straight and played to his new audience. 'There we go, Watson!' preached Holmes, his arm sweeping in a majestic arc. 'Once again, we solved the case and saved an innocent soul from the gallows. We are, once again, blessed by God!'

'A-ma-zing!' said Peter Adler. He turned to his soot-blackened friend. 'There you go, Roy; I have no doubt that we have just been privy to the satisfactory conclusion of a new mystery.' Roy nodded, grinning stupidly. Then, the good conductor turned to face us. 'Roy is also a follower of your adventures, sirs.' he said, almost in a whisper. 'He's a fanatic! He grabs my copy of *The Strand* as soon as I get it! Roy, here, would like to know if you would like to see the engine, as his *famous guest* and all that?'

I looked at Roy. 'It is obvious that YOU are not the driver. You will be the stoker, if I am not much mistaken?'

Holmes raised his eyebrows at me and shook his noble head in despair.

Roy doffed his cap to me. 'No, sir! I am the engine driver!'

I sprang up in my seat. 'Then who is driving the locomotive?!'

'My boy, George, sir! He can handle a 2-8-2 as well as anyone I know. He's a master of the valves.'

'So...' said Holmes, 'As I suspected... Boy George is driving this locomotive. He is four feet and eleven inches tall and twelve years of age.'

'That is correct, sir!' said Roy proudly, waving his cap around again, nearly catching Peter Adler's jaw as it plummeted towards the floor.

'But...how...j..j..just did you know that, sir?' stammered the bewildered conductor.

'I am afraid, gentlemen, that my simple methods must remain my own,' said Holmes.

'Well, is he twelve years old?' enquired Peter Adler.

'I dunno...' said Roy, thinking hard, his finger plugged into his mouth. 'Ten? Twelve? Who cares?'

I looked up. 'My goodness, sir, regardless of whether it is one or the other, is it not child labour?' Roy nodded enthusiastically. 'I love it! Come along, Holmes, shall we go and take a look?'

The master detective stood up and looked down his nose at me. 'I shall do just that, Watson,' he said, 'but it is just possible that you may be of some auxillary service in the investigation that lies before us. There are one or two minor points which were brought out in the inquest, and which are worth considering. You will stay here and read up on the case, as reported in the papers. Here...'

He tossed me a copy of the local Herefordshire paper and departed with the Sooties.

* * *

I settled myself down in the corner of the compartment and read the report on the murder, very carefully. It ran in this way:

"Mr. James McCartney, the only son of the deceased, was then called, and gave evidence as follows: 'I had been away from home for three days at Bristol, and had only just returned at the time of my arrival, and I was informed by the maid that he had driven over to Ross with John Cobb, the groom. Shortly after my return I heard the wheels of the trap in the yard, though I was not aware in which direction he was going. I then took my gun and strolled out towards the Boscombe Pool, with the intention of visiting the rabbit warren which is upon the other side. On my way I saw William Crowder, the gamekeeper, as he has stated in his evidence, but he is mistaken in thinking that I was following my father. I had no idea that he was in front of me. When about a hundred yards from the Pool I heard a cry of "Cooee!" which was a usual signal between my father and myself. I then hurried forward and found him standing by the Pool. He appeared to be much surprised at seeing me, and he asked me rather roughly what I was doing there. A conversation ensued, which led to high words, and almost to blows, for my father was a man of very violent temper. Seeing that his passion was becoming ungovernable, I left him, and returned towards Hatherley Farm. I had not gone more than one hundred and fifty yards, however, when I heard a hideous outcry behind me, which caused me to run back again. I found my father expiring on the ground, with his head terribly injured. I dropped my gun, and held him in my arms, but he almost instantly expired. I knelt beside him for some minutes, and then made my way to Mr. Turner's lodge-keeper, his house being the nearest, to ask for assistance. I saw no one near my father when I returned, and I have no idea how he came by his injuries. He was not a popular man, but he had, as far as I know, no active enemies. I know nothing further of the matter.'"

Then, there followed a rather tedious account of the proceedings at the Coroner's Court. It included a detailed transcript of the cross-questioning, in which the Coroner attempted to get to the bottom of the argument between father and son. He asked what his father's last words were before he died and the son was vague in his reply, saying only: "There was some allusion to a rat." When asked for the meaning of it, he added that he thought his father was "delirious." The Coroner then asked the witness what was the quarrel all about? But Mr. James McCartney refused point-blank to provide a suitable answer, or a reasonable explanation, saying that it was a private matter and bore no relevance to the murder itself. This distressed the Coroner somewhat. Then, he established with the witness that "Cooee!" was a personal family greeting, but James McCartney couldn't explain why his father had shouted it out before he was aware of his son's return from Bristol. Finally, the witness made it known to the Court that upon arrival at the side of his mortally wounded father, he had noticed a grey cloth – maybe a coat or maybe a plaid – laying on the ground a few yards away. Once his father had died, he turned to look for it, but it had disappeared. James McCartney could offer not explanation for its appearance or removal.

Sherlock Holmes opened the door. He was tinged with soot here and there, and he was a little dazed. 'I am not sure whether it is a good thing to be recognised by the general public quite so readily.'

I laughed. 'Why? Was it such a high price for a little fame?'

He sat himself down, back in the seat opposite me. 'Yes, indeed it is. I have never been asked so many inane questions by so many ordinary people in my life. And numerous autographs! As I made my escape, I was told that we lunch at Swindon. We shall be there in ten minutes.' He noticed *The Hereford Bugle* draped across my knees. 'Now, do you understand every nuance of the official proceedings in this case?'

'Yes, I think so,' I said, as I glanced down the column, 'I see that the Coroner in his concluding remarks was rather severe upon young McCartney. He calls attention, and with reason, to the discrepancy about his father having signalled to him before seeing him, also to his refusal to give details of his conversation with his father, and his singular account of his father's dying words. They are all, as he remarks, very much against the son.'

Holmes laughed softly to himself and stretched himself out upon the cushioned seat. 'Both you and the Coroner have been at some pains,' said he, 'to single out the very strongest points in the young man's favour. Don't you see that you alternately give him credit for having too much imagination and too little? Too little, if he could not invent a cause of quarrel which would give him the sympathy of the jury; too much, if he evolved from his own inner consciousness anything so *outré* as a dying reference to a rat, and the incident of the vanishing grey cloth. No, sir, I shall approach this case from the point of view that what this young man says is true, and we shall see whether that hypothesis will lead us. And now here is my pocket Petrarch. I shall throw my mind into a sonnet or two before we alight, and not another word shall I say of this case until we are on the scene of action.'

'Suit yourself!' I said, tartly. I did not like the way that he switched out of our analysis whenever it suited him. I knew what he was doing. He had decided to pontificate from within his sub-conscious, and he achieved that by scanning the lines of ancient Latin verse. Boring!

* * *

The luncheon in Swindon was very poor indeed. A shallow-grave toad-in-the-hole for me, and a poorly constructed cottage pie for Holmes, washed down with a second-rate Cotes du Rhône. During our mutual mastication, the great detective mentioned James McCartney's remark upon his arrest at Hatherley Farm that he was hardly surprised, and I responded with an ejaculation: 'You mean he confessed?!'

'No, not exactly. It was followed by a protestation of innocence.'

I chased a sausage around the plate whilst commenting about the stupidity of making such a remark in the first place.

'On the contrary,' remarked Holmes, 'it is the brightest rift which I can at present see in the clouds. However innocent he might be, he could not be such an absolute imbecile as not to see that the circumstances against him were very black indeed. Had he appeared surprised at his own arrest, or feigned indignation at it...'

'Like a grass snake?'

'No, Watson, not like a grass snake. What I am saying is that his frank acceptance of the situation marks him as either an innocent man, or else as a man of considerable self-restraint and firmness. His self-reproach and contrition, which are displayed in his remarks, appear to me to be the signs of a healthy mind rather than a guilty one.'

I shook my head. 'Many men have been hanged on far slighter evidence,' I remarked.

'So, they have. Speaking of which, somebody should be hanged for producing this pie.'

'And for serving these sausages. The cook must have minced up his Bethlehem Casuals to make these donkey's dicks!'

'Hmmm...' pondered the great detective. 'If there is a grim reality in our lives, Watson, it is the plight of English cuisine, which is not too dissimilar to that of James McCartney's situation.'

I was not quite sure what he meant by that, but I nodded and grunted in agreement anyway.

* * *

It was nearly four o'clock when we arrived at our destination. We had passed through the beautiful Stroud Valley, which was very shallow and, to me, was not deep enough to be a gorge, and so I named it a "georgie." We travelled over the broad gleaming Severn and found ourselves at the pretty little country town of Ross. A lean, ferret-like man, furtive and sly-looking, was waiting for us upon the platform. In spite of the light brown dustcoat and leather leggings, which he wore in deference to his rustic surroundings, I had no difficulty in recognising Lestrade, of Scotland Yard. With him we drove to the Hereford Arms, where a room had already been engaged for us.

'I have ordered a carriage,' said Lestrade, as we sat over a cup of tea. 'I knew your energetic nature, and that you would not be happy until you had been on the scene of the crime.'

'It was very nice and complimentary of you,' Holmes answered.

'It is not complimentary, Mr. Holmes. You will have to pay.'

'It is entirely a question of barometric pressure.'

Lestrade looked startled. 'I do not quite follow,' he said.

'How is the glass? Twenty-nine, I see. No wind, and not a cloud in the sky. I have a caseful of cigarettes here which need smoking, and the sofa is very much superior to the usual country hotel abomination. I do not think that it is probable that I shall use the carriage tonight.'

'Oh, I see…' remarked the police detective, with surprise in his voice. 'But you will still have to pay,' said Lestrade.

'Speak to the good Doctor about that, Lestrade. My mind will not be distracted, nor my brain cluttered by such ridiculous trivialities as money.'

Lestrade looked at me. I responded with the familiar, Agincourt-style, two-fingered salute. He laughed indulgently. 'I see that nothing changes… with either of you! Dear Mr. Holmes, the case is as plain as a pikestaff, and the more one goes into it the plainer it becomes. Still, of course, one can't refuse a lady, and such a very positive one too. She had heard of you, and would have your opinion, though I repeatedly told her that there was nothing which you could do which I had not already done.'

Holmes turned his gaze away from Lestrade and gurned a clown face at me. We laughed! Lestrade knew that he was being mocked; he sighed and rolled his eyes heavenwards. Before he could say anything, and just at that moment, a carriage drew up outside.

'Why, bless my soul! Here is Miss Turner now!'

He had hardly spoken before there standing in the room was one of the loveliest young women that I had ever seen in my life. Well, at least outside of London. Her violet eyes shining, her lips parted, a pink flush upon her cheeks, all thought of her natural reserve lost in her overpowering excitement and concern.

'Oh, Mr. Sherlock Holmes!' she cried, glancing from one to the other of us, and finally, with a woman's quick intuition fastening upon my companion, 'I am so glad that you have come. I want you to start upon your work knowing it, too. Never let yourself doubt upon

Miss Turner caught me red-handed waving at Lestrade in Agincourt style!

that point. Mr James McCartney and I have known each other since we were little children, and I know his faults as no one else does; but he is too tender-hearted to hurt a fly. Such a charge is absurd to anyone who really knows him.'

'I hope we may clear him, Miss Turner,' said Sherlock Holmes. 'You may rely upon my doing all that I can.'

'But you have read the evidence. You have formed some conclusions? Do you not see some loophole, some flaw? Do you not yourself think that he is innocent?'

'I think that it is very possible.'

'There now!' she cried, throwing back her head and looking defiantly at Lestrade. 'Did you hear that? He gives me hope!'

Lestrade shrugged his shoulders. 'I am afraid that my colleague has been a little quick in forming his conclusions,' he said.

'But he is right. Oh! I know that he is right. James never did it. And about his quarrel with his father, I am sure that the reason why he would not speak about it to the Coroner was because I was concerned in it.'

'In what way?' asked Holmes.

'It is no time for me to hide anything. James and his father had many disagreements about me. Mr. McCartney was very anxious that there should be a marriage between us. James and I have always loved each other as brother and sister, but of course he is young and has seen very little of life yet, and… and… well, he naturally did not wish to do anything like that yet. So, there were quarrels, and this, I am sure, was one of them.'

'And your father,' asked Holmes, 'was he in favour of such a union?'

'No, he was averse to it also. No one but Mr. McCartney was in favour of it.' A quick blush passed over her fresh face as Holmes shot one of his keen, questioning glances at her.

'Thank you for this information,' said he. 'May I see your father if I call tomorrow?'

'I am afraid the doctor won't allow it.'

'The doctor?'

'Yes, have you not heard? Poor Father has never been strong for years back, but this has broken him down completely. He has taken to his bed, and Dr. Willows says that he is a wreck, and that his nervous system is shattered. Mr. McCartney was the only man alive who had known Dad in the old days in Victoria.'

'Ha! In Victoria! That is important.'

'Yes, at the mines.'

'Quite so; at the gold mines, where, as I understand, Mr. Turner made his money.'

'Yes, certainly.'

'Thank you, Miss Turner. You have been of material assistance to me.'

'You will tell me if you have any news tomorrow. No doubt you will go to the prison to see James. Oh, if you do, Mr. Holmes, do tell him that I know him to be innocent.'

'I will, Miss Turner.'

'I must go home now, for Dad is very ill, and he misses me so if I leave him. Goodbye, and God help you in your undertaking.' She hurried from the room as impulsively as she had entered, and we heard the wheels of her carriage rattle off down the street. Damn!

I hadn't had even the whiff of a moment to engage her in a discussion about our fees. Meanwhile, Lestrade was doing his best to put his size twelves into the groin of the great detective's inquiry.

'I am ashamed of you, Holmes!' said Lestrade, all puffed up with peacock pride. 'Why should you raise up hopes which you are bound to disappoint? I am not over-tender of heart, but I call it cruel.'

'*Au contraire*, Lestrade,' Holmes retorted. 'I think that I see my way to clearing James McCartney. Have you an order to see him in prison?'

'Yes, but only for you and me.'

'What a cheek!' I exclaimed. 'What about me?'

'I must apologise to you, Doctor. I would have included you, but I wasn't aware of you joining Mr. Holmes on this trip.'

'But how?'

'I had heard that you had been sent to Coventry.' He smirked, probably at the childishness of the very thought of adults imposing trappism on one another.

'Holmes was also in Coventry, I'll have you know!' and then I rounded on Holmes, who must have been the informer, but the great detective was already high-tailing himself towards the hat rack and retrieving his new deerstalker. As I made my protestations, he looked over his shoulder and shouted:

'Inspector! I have reconsidered my resolution about going out. I hope that we shall still have time to take a carriage to Hereford and see James McCartney tonight.'

'We have ample time, Mr. Holmes,' he said, now laughing conceitedly. 'We must take a train first and then pick up the carriage. Ha! I knew that you wouldn't be able to resist embarking upon the adventure today.'

'Then let us do so, Inspector. Watson, I fear that you will find the next couple of hours or so very slow and boring, but I shall return soon enough.'

I walked down to the railway station with them. On the way, I had a chance to strike up a conversation with Lestrade, who was an amiable fellow. I asked him about their past, and how many times they had come together upon cases of such a grievous nature. He knew that he walked in the shadow of the great private detective and his most extraordinary methods. He liked Sherlock Holmes, apart from when he acted in a condescending way, belittling the official police force and its limited resources. I took the opportunity of picking up on the matter of resources. We had a frank discussion about money and the value of Holmes's guidance.

On the platform I bid farewell to Holmes. He winked at me and drew the ear flaps down on his new cloth cap as he climbed into the carriage. I started laughing and shouted out. 'The Lestrade!' after which the Inspector turned and looked at me quizzically and said: 'Yes, Doctor? What is it?' But Holmes simply reached out, grabbed him by the collar and drew him inside.

After they had departed, I then wandered through the streets of the little town, finally returning to the hotel, where I lay upon the sofa and tried to interest myself in a yellow-backed novel. The puny plot of the story was so thin, however, when compared to the deep mystery through which we were groping, and I found my attention wander so constantly from the fiction to the fact, that I at last flung it across the room and gave myself up entirely to a consideration of the events of the day. Supposing that this unhappy young man's story was absolutely true, then what hellish thing, what absolutely unforeseen and extraordinary calamity, could have occurred between the time when he parted from his father and the moment when, drawn back by his screams, he rushed into the glade? It was something terrible and deadly. What could it be? Hmmm! Hold on, I was a Doctor of Medicine! Might not the nature of the injuries reveal something to my highly tuned professional instincts? I jumped up and rang the bell. I called for the weekly county paper to be given to me at once! And it was. I found that it contained a verbatim account of the inquest. In the surgeon's deposition it was stated that the posterior third of the left parietal bone and the left half of the occipital bone had been shattered by a heavy blow from a blunt weapon. I marked the spot upon my own head. Clearly such a blow must have been struck from behind. That was to some extent in favour of the accused, as when seen quarrelling he was face to face with his father. Still, it did not go for very much, for the older man might have turned his back before the blow fell. Still, it might be worthwhile to call Holmes's attention to it, even though he was only a Doctor of Chemistry. Ha! Then, there was a peculiar dying reference to a rat. What could that mean? It could not be a delirium because I knew that a man dying from a sudden blow does not commonly become delirious. No, it was more likely to be an attempt to explain how he met his fate. But what could it indicate? I cudgelled my brains to find some possible explanation. And then the incident of the grey cloth, seen by young McCartney. If that were true, the murderer must have dropped some part of his dress, presumably his overcoat, in his flight, and must have had the hardihood to return and carry it away at the instant when the son was kneeling with his back turned not a dozen paces off. What a tissue of mysteries and improbabilities the whole thing was! I do not wonder at Lestrade's opinion, and yet I had so much faith in Sherlock Holmes's insight that I could not lose hope as long as every fresh fact seemed to strengthen his conviction of young McCartney's innocence.

It was late before Sherlock Holmes returned. He came back alone, for Lestrade was staying in lodgings in the town. He removed the deerstalker and admired it lovingly before restoring the ear flaps to the elevated position.

'This cloth hat, Doctor,' he said, 'is a marvellous creation. Throughout the whole journey to Hereford prison and back again, Lestrade battled on to me with his theories about this case. Thanks to the deerstalker...'

'The Lestrade!' I corrected.

'Thanks to The Lestrade I heard hardly a word.'

'Marvellous, Holmes! Maybe you should use it on all of the future cases where the Inspector has been put in charge?'

'Ha! That, Watson, is one of your finer suggestions and one that I shall adhere to.' He walked over to the barometer and gave it a tap. 'The glass still keeps very high,' he remarked. He went to sit down. 'It is of importance that it should not rain before we are able to go over the ground. On the other hand, a man should be at his very best and keenest for such nice work as that, and I did not wish to do it when fagged by a long journey. I have seen young McCartney.'

In a confined space the 'Lestrade' deerstalker needed additional muffling.

'Quite so, Holmes. And what did you learn from him?'

'Nothing.'

'Could he throw no light?'

'None at all. I was inclined to think at one time that he knew who had done it, and was screening him or her, but I am convinced now that he is as puzzled as everyone else. He is not a very quick-witted youth, though comely to look at, and, I should think, sound at heart.'

'I cannot admire his taste,' I remarked, 'if it is indeed a fact that he was averse to a marriage with so charming a young lady as this Miss Turner.'

'Well, Watson, may I remind you that we can hardly trust your judgment on the subject of a lady's appearance after you married Miss Mary Morstan, who was, as it turned out, Mark, the female impersonator!'*

'Oh ha, ha, ha, Holmes! May I remind you that you confessed to knowing all about my bride's deception on your first encounter with...er... Mark, and you still let me go ahead with the marriage *and* take him away on a honeymoon!'

Holmes laughed out loud. 'I did, Watson! I did! But remember – a joke is never truly funny unless the victim is hurt or loses money. This particular ruse ticked both of the boxes; hence we still chuckle about it now. Ha!'

He might chuckle but I certainly did not! I gave him my most surly of glares, which made him chortle like drain. He put up his arms in front of his face. 'Please, Watson! Not the death-stare!'

---

* see previous adventure: *'A Balls-Up In Bohemia'*

'Holmes, it is late. Can we just return to the story of James McCartney? I have read more of the incident in the paper, even the medical report, and I am genuinely fascinated by this case.'

'Certainly. About your supposition of earlier, I can put you right. This fellow is madly, insanely in love with Miss Turner, but some two years ago, when he was only a lad, and before he really knew her, for she had been away five years at a boarding-school, what does the idiot do but get into the clutches of a barmaid in Bristol!'

'He clutched the bristols on a barmaid, Holmes?'

'That I cannot be sure of, Watson. But it gets worse – he then marries her at the registry office!'

'NO!'

'Indeed, he does! No one knows a word of the matter, but you can imagine how maddening it must be to him to be upbraided for not doing what he would give his very eyes to do, but what he knows to be absolutely impossible. It was sheer frenzy of this sort which made him throw his hands up into the air when his father, at their last interview, was goading him on to propose to Miss Turner. On the other hand, he had no means of supporting himself, and his father, who was by all accounts a very hard man, and would have thrown him over utterly had he known the truth. It was with his barmaid wife that he had spent the last three days in Bristol, and his father did not know where he was. Make note of that point. It is of great importance. Good has come out of evil, however, for the barmaid, finding from the papers that he is in serious trouble, and likely to be hanged, has thrown him over utterly, and has written to him to say that she has a husband already in the Bermuda Dockyard.'

'A proper tart!'

'Luckily for young James McCartney, yes. Now there is no legal tie between them. I think that that bit of news has consoled young McCartney for all that he has suffered.'

'But if he is innocent, who has done it?'

'Ah! Who? I would call your attention very particularly to two points. One is that the murdered man had an appointment with someone at the Pool, and that the someone could not have been his son, for his son was away, and he did not know when he would return. The second is that the murdered man was heard to cry "Cooee!" before he knew that his son had returned. Those are the crucial points upon which the case depends. And now let us talk about something more trivial, if you please, and we shall leave the minor points until tomorrow.'

* * *

There was no rain, as Holmes and the hotel barometer had foretold, and the morning broke bright and cloudless. At nine o'clock Lestrade called for us with the carriage, and we set off for Hatherley Farm and Boscombe Pool.

'There is serious news this morning,' Lestrade observed. 'It is said that Mr. Turner, of the Hall, is so ill that his life is despaired of.'

'He is an elderly man, I presume?'

'About sixty, but his constitution has been shattered by his life abroad, and he has been in failing health for some time. This business has had a very bad effect upon him. He was an old friend of McCartney's, and, I may add, a great benefactor to him, for I have learned that he gave him Hatherley Farm rent free.'

'Indeed?! That is interesting,' said Holmes.

'Oh, yes! And in a hundred other ways he has helped him. Everybody about here speaks of his kindness to him.'

'Really! Does it not strike you as a little singular that this McCartney, who appears to have had little of his own fortune, and to have been under such obligations to Turner, should still talk of marrying his son to Turner's daughter, who is presumably heiress to the estate, and that in such a very cocksure manner, as if it was merely a case of a decent proposal and all else would follow? It is the stranger since we know that Turner himself was averse to the idea. The daughter told us as much. Do you not deduce something from that?'

'We have got to do all of his deductions and inferences, whether they are relevant to the case or not' said Lestrade, winking at me.

'Yes, but there is a reason for that,' I said. 'It is because he is always right.' That made Lestrade recoil! I blew him a silent kiss. That made him recoil even further! His eyes fluttered and blinked for a moment or two. Then, he composed himself again.

'I find it hard enough to tackle the facts, Holmes, without flying away after theories and fancies.'

'I am sure of that!' said Holmes demurely. 'You do find it very hard to tackle the facts.'

Take that, stupid copper! Lestrade looked stricken, but hardly knocked out. He was thick-skinned. At first, he gaped at the great detective, and then something came into his head because suddenly he smiled warmly at him. 'Anyhow, I have grasped one fact which you seem to find it difficult to get hold of,' exclaimed Lestrade.

Riposte!

'And that is?' said Holmes, with total wonder in his voice whilst reaching up for the corded bow that fastened the flaps on his deerstalker.

'That McCartney senior met his death from McCartney junior, and that all theories to the contrary are the merest moonshine.'

'Is that it?' said Holmes, flashing his eyes at me for a second. A-ha! That was the signal.

'Yes, Mr. Holmes, that is it,' confirmed Lestrade.

'Lestrade?' I asked, and hung on for a second, for dramatic effect... 'Is THAT it?'

'Why, Dr. Watson... Yes! THAT is it!'

'Come, come, Lestrade...' protested Holmes. 'That cannot be it... Is THAT IT?'

I jumped up and goaded myself into a trembling temper. I shook my fist in Lestrade's face. 'You CANNOT tell me THAT IS IT!' I shouted.

'THAT IS IT, DOCTOR! screamed Lestrade, rising up angrily out of his seat, his face reddening like a baboon's posterior. 'AND THAT IS FINAL!' he blasted, with all of his might.

(* see previous adventure: *'The Mysterious Case of Mr. Gingernuts'*)

Then, silence! An angel passed through the compartment. We calmed ourselves and sat down again. We looked at one another. Then, Holmes glanced at me in a certain way, and we fell about laughing. Ah, it was so good to do it again! We had not had chance to play out that little routine of ours for a few weeks now, not since that tiresome red-headed chap bored us to death about losing his overpaid job.* To Lestrade's credit, it didn't take long for him to realise that he had been taken for a ride, and soon he joined in with the merriment by laughing along with us. He even added to the fun by chastising us for our folly with mock scolding and bashing us playfully with his trilby.

'Well,' said Holmes, 'I can assure you, Lestrade, that moonshine is brighter than fog! And, by the way, unless I am very much mistaken, is this not Hatherley Farm upon the left?'

'Yes, that is it,' the policeman replied. It was a widespread, comfortable-looking building, two-storied, slate-roofed, with great yellow blotches of lichen upon the grey walls. The drawn blinds and the smokeless chimneys, however, gave it a stricken look, as though the weight of this horror lay upon it. We called at the door, when the maid, at Holmes's request, showed us the boots which her master wore at the time of his death, and also a pair of the son's, though not the pair which he had then had. Confused, dear reader? You should be! Anyway, having measured these boots and shoes carefully, from seven or eight different points, Holmes desired to be led to the courtyard, from which we all followed the winding track which led to Boscombe Pool.

As we approached the Pool, he came to a halt. He raised his arms to his cloth hat. His long white fingers untied the cord; the flaps dropped down and flattened over his ears. He re-tied them tight under his chin. Now, he nodded to me, and then he was off! On the hunt! Sherlock Holmes was transformed when he was hot upon such a scent as this. Men who had only known the quiet thinker and logician of Baker Street would have failed to recognise him. His face flushed and darkened. His brows were drawn into two hard lines, while his eyes shone out from beneath them with steely glitter. His face was bent downwards, his shoulders bowed, his lips compressed, and the veins stood out like whipcord in his long, sinewy neck. His nostrils seemed to dilate with a purely animal lust for the chase, and his mind was so absolutely concentrated upon the matter before him, that a question or remark fell unheeded upon his ears, or at the most only provoked a quick, impatient snarl in reply. Swiftly and silently he made his way along the track which ran through the meadows, and so by way of the woods to the Boscombe Pool. Lestrade and I strolled along behind, giving him plenty of room. It was damp, marshy ground, as is all that district, and there were marks along of many feet, both upon the path and amid the short grass which bounded it on either side. Sometimes Holmes would hurry on, sometimes stop dead, and once he made quite a little *détour* into the meadow. We followed him in, noticed him reach through his unbuttoned fly and release his cock-a-doodle-doo, turned around, and walked back to the path. When he had finished relieving himself, he resumed his journey to the Pool. Once again, we followed behind him, the detective indifferent and contemptuous, while I watched my friend with the interest which sprang from the conviction that every one of his actions was directed towards a definite end.

The Boscombe Pool, which is a little reed-girt sheet of water some fifty yards across, is situated at the boundary between the Hatherley Farm and the private park of the wealthy Mr. Turner. Above the woods which lined it upon the farther side we could see the red jutting pinnacles which marked the site of the rich landowner's dwelling. On the Hatherley side of the Pool the woods grew very thick, and there was a narrow belt of sodden grass twenty paces across, between the edge of the trees and the reeds which lined the lake. Lestrade showed us the exact spot at which the body had been found, and indeed, so moist was the ground, that I could plainly see the traces which had been left by the fall of the stricken man. To Holmes, as I could see by his eager face and peering eyes, very many other things were to be read upon the trampled grass. He ran around, like a dog who is picking up a scent, and then turned upon my companion, lifting the deerstalker flaps.

'What did you go into the Pool for?' he asked.

'I fished about with a rake. I thought there might be some weapon or other trace. BUT, HOW DID YOU KNOW?!'

'Oh tsk, tut and fiddle-dee-dee! I have no time for an explanation, Lestrade. That left foot of yours with its inwards twist is all over the place. A mole could trace it, and there it vanishes among the reeds. Oh, how simple it all would have been had I been here before they came like a herd of buffalo and wallowed all over it. Here is where the party with the lodge-keeper came, and they have covered all the tracks for six or eight feet

Not even glissading on McCartney's dog's turd distracted Holmes during his forensic work!

around the body. But there are three separate tracks of the same feet.' He drew out a lens and lay down upon his waterproof to have a better view, talking all the time rather to himself than to us. 'These are young McCartney's feet. Twice he was walking, and once he ran swiftly so that the soles are deeply marked, and the heels hardly visible. That bears out his story. He ran when he saw his father on the ground. Then here are the father's feet as he paced up and down. What is this, then? It is the butt end of the gun as the son stood listening. And this? Ha-ha! What have we here? Tiptoes! Tiptoes! Square, too, quite unusual boots! They come, they go, they come again – of course that was for the cloak. Now where did they come from?' He ran up and down, sometimes losing, sometimes finding the track, until we were well within the edge of the wood and under the shadow of a great beech, the largest tree in the neighbourhood. Holmes traced his way to the farther side of this. He lay down once more upon his face. We heard a little cry. Lestrade turned to me.

'Oh dear! I seem to remember McCartney's dog depositing a pile of doo-doos over there,' said Lestrade.

'No, Lestrade' I replied with certainty, 'that is not Holmes glissading upon a dog turd. That is his cry of satisfaction.'

'Huh! I suppose you would know!' he muttered. 'You two being holed up together in that tiny apartment together...'

'Inspector, you could not be further from the truth. The apartment is more than adequate in size and accommodation for our needs.'

'That's not... well, what I meant was, you would be more in tune with his mannerisms.'

'Yes, I am!' He gave me a startled gape at the supposed point-blank honesty. I pointed at Holmes. 'Look now! He has remained over there for a long time. He is turning over the leaves and dried sticks. He is gathering up dust into an envelope. He examines with his lens, not only the ground, but even the bark of the tree, as far as he can reach. And hark! Can you hear? Each time he finds something, he gives the same cry, the cry of satisfaction, not that of a man running into a dog turd, or, for that matter, any sordid insinuations about our relationship that you can dream up, Inspector!'

He looked quite piqued, so that spiked his inquisitiveness! We watched Holmes in silence. A jagged stone was lying among the moss, and this also Holmes carefully examined and retained. Then he followed a pathway through the wood until he came to the high road, where all traces were lost. Then, he returned to us with a nasty streak of dog mess trowelled along his coat sleeve.

'It has been a case of considerable interest,' he remarked, returning to his natural manner. 'I fancy that this grey house on the right must be the lodge. I think that I will go in and have a word with Morahan, and perhaps write a little note. Having done that, we may drive back to our luncheon. You may walk to the cab, and I shall be with you presently.'

It was about ten minutes before we regained our cab, and drove back into Ross, Holmes still carrying with him the stone, which he had picked up in the wood, and stinking of you-know-what.

'This may interest you, Lestrade,' he remarked, holding it out. 'The murder was done with it.'

'I see no marks.'

'There are none.'

'How do you know?'

'The grass was growing under it. It had only lain there a few days. There was no sign of a place whence it had been taken. It corresponds with the injuries. There is no sign of any other weapon.'

'And the murderer?'

'Is a tall man, left-handed, limps with the right leg, wears thick-soled shooting boots and a grey cloak, smokes Indian cigars, uses a cigar-holder, and carries a blunt penknife in his pocket. There are several other indications, but that may be enough to aid us in our search.'

Lestrade laughed. 'I am afraid that I am still a sceptic,' he said. 'Theories are all very well, but we have to deal with a hard-headed British jury.'

'*Nous verrons,*' answered Holmes calmly, and goodness knows why he was speaking in Frog, but luckily, he continued in our native tongue. 'You work your own method,' he continued, 'and I shall work mine. I shall be busy this afternoon and shall probably return to London by the evening train.'

'And leave your case unfinished?'

'No, it is finished.'

'But the mystery?'

'What mystery? It is solved.'

'Who was the criminal then?'

'The gentleman I describe.'

'But who is he?'

'Surely it would not be difficult to find out? This is not such a populous neighbourhood.'

Lestrade shrugged his shoulders. 'I am a practical man,' he said, 'and I really cannot undertake to go about the country looking for a left-handed gentleman with a gammy leg. I should become the laughing-stock of Scotland Yard.'

'If you hang an innocent man Lestrade, you will be more than just a laughing-stock. You will be an accomplice to murder and might be unemployed.'

'So there!' I added. Lestrade blanched. Holmes threw me an appreciative glance and turned back to the policeman. 'I have given you the chance,' Holmes said quietly. 'Here are your lodgings. Goodbye. I shall drop you a line before I leave.'

* * *

We left a distraught-looking Lestrade on the side of the road. Just as our cab set off, he looked up at us from the verge on the side of the road and I gave him another, subtle flick of the Agincourt fingers. He didn't react.

We drove to our hotel, where we found lunch upon the table. Holmes was silent and buried in thought, with a pained expression upon his face, as one who finds himself in a perplexing situation.

'Look here, Watson,' he said, when the cloth was cleared; 'just sit down in this chair and let me preach to you for a little while. I don't quite know what to do, and I should value your advice. Light a cigar and let me expound.'

Ah! So, it was Dr. Watson, the essential sounding-board at-the-ready! 'Pray, do so, I said,' with a wry smile upon my face and sitting myself down in one of the luxurious sofas. My goodness it was comfortable being essential!

'Well, now, in considering this case there are two points about young McCartney's narrative which struck us both instantly, although they impressed me in his favour and you against him. One was the fact that his father should, according to his account, cry "Cooee!" before seeing him. The other was his singular reference to a rat. He mumbled several words, you understand, but that was all that caught the son's ear. Now from this double point our research must commence, and we will begin it by presuming that what the lad says is absolutely true.'

'What of this "Cooee!" then?'

'Well, obviously it could not have been meant for the son. The son, as far as he knew, was in Bristol. It was mere chance that he was within earshot. The "Cooee!" was meant to attract the attention of whoever it was that he had the appointment with. But "Cooee!" is a distinctly Australian cry, and one which is used between Australians. There is a strong presumption that the person whom McCartney expected to meet at Boscombe Pool was someone who had been in Australia.'

'I find it staggering that these Australians cannot address each other properly. What is the matter with "Good morning" or "Good afternoon," or even the ghastly greeting of: "Hello?"'

Holmes sighed. His shoulders dropped in anguish. He peered at me from under his eyebrows. 'Watson, isn't it obvious? It is not the emigrants like McCartney and Turner that this address is derived from; it is an expression picked up by them from the native Australian. I am referring to the Aborigine.'

'Ah! The Abo!' I remarked. 'I have heard of them, from when I was in the army.'

'A derogatory nickname for a remarkable human being. The Aborigine is a hunter! And he is a survivor! Perchance, the British and Irish colonists have made a hard life for the Aborigines, notwithstanding that unpleasant nickname.'

'Well, Holmes, if that's what you have heard... Some of my old regiment chums wouldn't agree with that sentiment. They would go hunting with the Abos.'

'They would go hunting *for* the Aboriginals, Watson! Vile! Quite vile! But "Cooee" comes from the Dharug region of New South Wales, and that's all that matters for this case. In this instance, it had been adopted by the McCartneys for their own special use.'

'Yes. Absolutely. What of the rat, then?'

Sherlock Holmes took a folded paper from his pocket and flattened it out on the table. 'This is a map of the Colony of Victoria,' he said. 'I wired to Bristol for it last night.' He put his hand over part of the map. 'What do you read?' he asked.

'ARAT.' I read.

'And now?' He raised his hand.

'BALLARAT.'

'Quite so. That was the word the man uttered, and of which his son only caught the last two syllables. He was trying to utter the name of his murderer. So-and-so of Ballarat.'

'You are wonderful!' I exclaimed.

'It is obvious. And now, you see, I had narrowed the field down considerably. The possession of a grey garment was a third point which, granting the son's statement to be correct, was a certainty. We have come now out of a mere vagueness to the definite conception of an Australian from Ballarat with a grey cloak.'

'Certainly.'

'And one who was at home in the district, for the Pool can only be approached by the farm or by the estate, where strangers could hardly wander.'

'Quite so.'

'Then comes our expedition of today. By an examination of the ground I gained the trifling details which I gave to that imbecile Lestrade, as to the personality of the criminal.'

'But how did you gain them by trifling?' I avoided any gibes about traditional English puddings.

'Don't be silly, Watson! You know my method. It is founded upon the observance of trifles.'

'This man's height I know that you might roughly judge from the length of his stride. His boots, too, might be told from their traces.'

'Yes, and they were peculiar boots.'

'But his lameness?'

'The impression of his right foot was always less distinct than his left. He put less weight upon it. Why? Because he limped. He was lame.'

'So, this chap has got a leg down, as we would say in the mess. But what about his left-handedness?'

'You were yourself struck by the nature of the injury as recorded by the surgeon at the inquest. The blow was struck from immediately behind, and yet was upon the left side. Now, how can that be unless it were by a left-handed man? He had stood behind that tree during the interview between the father and son. He had even smoked there. I found the ash of a cigar, which my special knowledge of tobacco ashes enabled me to pronounce as an Indian cigar. I have, as you know, devoted some attention to this, and written a little monograph on the ashes of 140 different varieties of pipe, cigar, and cigarette tobacco.'

'Only a monograph, and not a treatise, Holmes! My, you are slipping!'

'Shut up, Watson. I haven't finished; one day it will be treatise. Having found the ash, I then looked around and discovered the stump among the moss where he had tossed it. It was an Indian cigar...'

'Huzzah!'

'...of the variety which are rolled in Rotterdam. I could, for instance, see that the end had not been in his mouth. Therefore, he used a holder. The tip had been cut off, not bitten off, but the cut was not a clean one, so I deduced a blunt penknife.'

'I perceive you have drawn a net around this man from which he cannot escape, and you have saved an innocent human being's life as truly as if you had cut the cord which was hanging him. I see the direction in which all this points. So, the culprit is?'

'Mr. Gerald Turner!' cried the hotel receptionist, opening the door of our sitting room, and ushering in a visitor.

The man who entered was a strange and impressive figure. His slow, limping step and bowed shoulders gave the appearance of decrepitude, and yet his hard, deep-lined, craggy features, and his enormous limbs showed that he was possessed of unusual strength of body and of character. His tangled beard, grizzled hair, and outstanding, drooping eyebrows combined to give an air of dignity and power to his appearance, but his face was of an ashen white, whilst his lips and the corners of his nostrils were tinged with a shade of blue. It was clear to me at a glance that he was in the grip of some deadly chronic disease.

'Pray sit down on the sofa,' said Holmes gently. 'You had my note?'

'Yep, cobber!' said Turner, with a tremendously inflected lift to his second word. 'The lodge-keeper brought it up to me. "Old Lodgie," I call him!'

Oof! What style of accent was that?! I had never encountered an Australian at close quarters before. I caught Holmes's eye and he raised his brows devilishly before Turner continued with his next comment.

'Anyway... you said that you wished to see me here. Something about avoiding a scandal?'

'I thought people would talk if I went to the Hall.'

'Yeah, mate, but why did you want to see me, eh?' He looked across at my companion with despair in his eyes, as though the question were already answered. I was despairing as well, with that infernal end-of-sentence inflection. It was enough to drive anyone to distraction!

'Yes,' said Holmes, answering the look of the man rather than his words, 'it is so. I know all about McCartney and what took place between you.'

The old man sank his face in his hands. 'God help me!' he cried. 'But I would not have let that young man come to any harm! I give you my word that I would have spoken out if it went against him at the Assizes.'

'I am glad to hear you say so,' said Holmes gravely.

'I would have spoken out by now, had it not been for my dear girl. It would break her heart – it will break *my* heart when she hears that I am arrested.'

'I am no official agent. I am a private detective, engaged by your daughter, who required my presence here. I am acting in her interests. Young McCartney must be got off, however.'

'I am a very sick man,' said old Turner. 'I have had diabetes for years. My doctor says it is a question whether I shall live a month.'

I stood up. 'I am a doctor, sir!' I announced, 'and a London one at that. Let me give you a second opinion.'

'Not now, Watson...'

Turner was old and he was rich! At five guineas a time, I could make some money out of this caper around the country after all. 'No, Holmes,' I said, 'there is no time like the present!'

I strode over to where Mr. Turner was sitting and stood opposite him. I cradled his face with both hands and pulled his jaw down. I could hear the great detective sighing slowly as I turned the Australian's open mouth towards the daylight afforded by the large panes of the bay window. 'Now, Mr. Turner... say AAAAAH!'

'Watson!' I looked up and around at Sherlock Holmes. 'I am sure you have the best of intentions and Mr. Turner, here, appreciates your concern, but this is not necessary.'

Mr. Turner wriggled hard, trying to catch a glimpse of Holmes, but I held him in position, trying to get a birds-eye view of his epiglottis. Then, suddenly, he gargled: 'GIT THIS FRIGGIN' MANIAC OFF MY...' And then he wrenched free, stood up in a trice, and Wallop! He punched me on the chin! I went out like a candle...

According to Holmes, I was only unconscious for a minute, but it felt like much longer. As I came to, the first words I recalled were from Gerald Turner speaking to Sherlock Holmes.

'I am a dying man, and I know that for a fact. I would rather die under my own roof than in a jail.'

Holmes rose from his chair. As he walked by me, he reached down with his long arm to give me a hand up with a 'welcome back, Watson.' He sat down at the table, with his pen in his hand and a bundle of paper before him. 'Just tell us the truth,' he said. 'I shall jot down the facts, you will sign it and Watson here can witness it.'

'It will be my pleasure,' I said, still checking my jaw and coming to my senses. 'Once I can see straight again.'

Mr. Turner looked up at me from his seat. 'Sorry about that, cobber. Where I come from, we tend to get what we want by using our fists, not fancy words.'

I stared at him, dead seriously. 'That is all very easy for you to say, Mr. Turner, but I was examining you. Just what you would have done if I had been checking you for a hernia?' We all laughed like drains at the thought of me cupping the old man's testicles! After a minute or so, Holmes said he was ready to start writing and added: 'I shall be able to produce this confession at any time to save young McCartney.'

'That's fine, mate,' said Turner, 'but it's a question whether I shall live long enough to attend the Assizes. It matters little to me, but I should wish to spare Alice the shock. And now I will make the thing clear to you; I'll tell you the whole story. It has been a long time in the acting but will not take me long to tell.'

I sat down on the sofa again, feeling much better. Holmes was sat at the table, poised for action of the secretarial kind.

'First of all,' said the old man, 'you didn't know this dead man, McCartney. Neither of you met him. He was the devil incarnate. I tell you that. God keep you out of the clutches of such a man as he. His grip has been upon me these past twenty years, and he has blasted my life. I'll tell you first how I came to be in his power.

'It was in the early 'sixties at the diggings. I was a young chap then, hot-blooded and reckless, ready to turn my hand to anything; I got among bad companions, took to drink, had no luck with my claim, took to the bush, and, in a word, became what you would call over here a highway robber. There were six of us, and we had a wild, free life of it, sticking up a station from time to time, or stopping the wagons on the road to the diggings. Black Jack of Ballarat was the name I went under.'

'That's odd, I said, 'considering your name is Gerald?'

'Shut up, Watson! Pray, continue, Mr. Turner...'

'Have a heart, Doctor! Black Gerald, or Black Gerry, doesn't really work, does it? It has no ring to it.'

I nodded my acceptance of his logic.

'As I was saying, Mr. Holmes, I called myself Black Jack and our party of desperate robbers is still remembered in the colony as the Ballarat Gang. Anyway, one day a gold convoy came down from Ballarat to Melbourne, and we lay in wait for it and attacked it. There were six troopers and six of us, so it was a close thing, but we emptied four of their saddles in the first volley. Three of our boys were killed, however, before we got the swag. I put my pistol to the head of the wagon-driver, who was this very man McCartney. I wish to the Lord I had shot him then, but I spared him, though I saw his wicked little eyes fixed on my face, as though to remember every feature. We got away with the gold, became wealthy men, and made our way over to England without being suspected. There I parted from my old pals and I determined to settle down to a quiet and respectable life. I bought this estate, which chanced to be on the market, and I set myself to do a little good with my money, to make up for the way in which I had earned it. I married too, and though my wife died young, she left me my dear little Alice. Even when she was just a baby her wee hand seemed to lead me down the right path as nothing else has ever done. In a word, I turned over a new leaf, and did my best to make up for the past. All was going well when McCartney laid his grip upon me.

'I had gone up to town about an investment, and I met him in Regent Street with hardly a coat to his back or a boot to his foot.'

'"Here we are, Jack," says he, touching me on the arm; "we'll be as good as a family to you. There's two of us, me and my son, and you will have the keeping of us. If you don't, I shall reveal your true identity.

It's a fine, law-abiding country in England, and there's always a policeman within hail."'

'A supposition that might be a threat, providing the policeman isn't Inspector Lestrade!' quipped Holmes. We both laughed whilst Turner looked on in wonder, until a flash of recognition hit him between the eyes.

'Oh! You mean that possum policeman? Ha! Yes, he seems to be off track, poor bloke! Anyway, back to my story... This McCartney and his nipper came down to the West Country and there they have lived rent free on my best land ever since. There was no shaking them off, no rest for me, no peace, no forgetfulness; turn where I would, there was his cunning, grinning face at my elbow. It grew worse as Alice grew up, for he soon saw I was more afraid of her knowing my past than of a revelation to the police. Whatever he wanted he must have, and whatever it was I gave him without question: land, money, houses, until at last he asked for a thing which I could not give. He asked for Alice to be James's bride.

'His son you see, had grown up, and so had my girl, and as I was known to be in weak health, it seemed a fine stroke to him that his lad should step into the whole property. But this time I was unwilling to agree to his demand; I would not have his cursed stock mixed with mine, not that I had any dislike to the lad, but his blood was in him, and that was enough. I stood my ground, even when McCartney threatened me. I braved him to do his worst. We agreed to meet at the Pool midway between our houses to talk it over.

'When I went down there, I found him talking to his son, so I smoked a cigar, and waited behind a tree until he should be alone. But as I listened to his talk all that was black and bitter in me seemed to come uppermost. He was urging his son to marry my daughter with as little regard for what she might think, as if she were a slut from off the streets.'

Holmes and I exchanged glances. Neither of us liked the use of that word when it referred to our client, especially as one as lovely as Miss Turner. We marked his card but didn't interrupt the old Australian from telling his story.

'It drove me mad to think that I and all that I held most dear should be in the power of such a man as this. Could I not snap the bond? I was already a dying and desperate man. Though clear of mind and fairly strong of limb, I knew that my own fate was sealed. But my memory and my girl! Both could be saved, if I could but silence that foul tongue. I did it, Mr. Holmes. I would do it again. Deeply as I have sinned, I have led a life of martyrdom to atone for it. But that my girl should be entangled in the same meshes which held me was more than I could suffer. I selected a rock from the ground, picked it up and struck him down. Wallop! Wallop! Wallop! I stoved in his brains, as if he had been some foul and venomous beast. His cry brought back his son; but I had gained the cover of the wood, though I was forced to go back to fetch the cloak which I had dropped in my flight. That is the true story, gentlemen, of all that occurred.'

'It is murder most foul. Have you finished, sir?' enquired Holmes, as he stood up and pocketed the pen.

'Yes, mate! That's about the size of it.'

'In which case... INSPECTOR! COME!' There was a rustling and a banging and Lestrade appeared from the adjoining room with two burly policemen

*Mr. Turner liked the image of being a tough,
cold-blooded killer but I wondered what really happened
down by the pool was down to one of the dog turds ...*

at his side. He had been listening discreetly to every word we had uttered, thus condemning Turner to eternal damnation. In fairness, I would have liked to say something on behalf of the confessor because he had been gulled into a false sense of security, but it was too late. He had spilled the beans. Turner looked distraught, his face drooping down, his eyes forced wide open by the surprise of such a turn of events. 'But Mr. Holmes,' he begged, 'I had thought that we had an understanding? Why do you seek me this injustice?'

'Injustice? This *is* justice, Mr. Turner! Is it not plainly obvious? You confessed to killing McCartney and many more people too. You are a cold-blooded killer. A murderer, sir! You cannot expect leniency or clemency from anyone.'

'Look on the bright side,' I said. 'You will be dispatched humanely by the hangman, sparing you a lingering and painful death by some unpredictable cancer growth.'

'Oh thanks a bundle!' he cried.

'And I have spared you the ignominy of you spending your last days in jail,' said Holmes. 'Besides, you will soon have to answer for your deeds at a higher court than the Assizes. Lestrade! Take him away!'

Mr. Turner was seized by the policemen, one on each arm. His whole frame dropped to half of its height, a man beaten by his own historical crimes, all coming home to roost at once.

'Farewell then,' said the old man solemnly. Tottering and shaking in all his giant frame, he stumbled slowly from the room. 'Having tricked me into a confession I suppose your own deathbeds, when they come, will be easier for you to lie in.'

'They certainly will!' cried Holmes, and I followed up by swinging a boot into his posterior, as was my habit. 'So, on your way, you dastardly, cowardly villain!' I shouted at him.

Once he was gone, the great detective sighed deeply. 'God help us!' said Holmes. 'A person goes around murdering people, at will, and he expects to escape the hangman's noose, just because he has become old and ill! I ask you, Watson, Lestrade – what type of inhuman world are we living in?'

'Quite!' I nodded in agreement, alongside the hapless Inspector.

'Thank you and goodbye, Mr. Holmes,' said Lestrade, preparing to leave. 'You have been most helpful to me on this case, and despite all those derogatory remarks that I overheard during that confession, I have been most fortunate of your presence here. You have saved me from a more serious embarrassment. Imagine if we had gone ahead with the execution of James McCartney?'

'If YOU had gone ahead with it, Inspector; not "we." Anyway, I am delighted to be of service, and I bid you *au revoir*, because it is only a matter of time before our paths cross once again.'

'Until the next time, Mr. Holmes, replied Lestrade, lifting his trilby to us as he headed towards the door. I cleared my throat loudly and he stopped to look round at me. 'Doctor?'

'Have you not forgotten something, Inspector? Remember our conversation on the way to the station yesterday?'

Lestrade spun his hat around in his hands and forced a grin onto his face as he looked up. 'I won't forget to lodge a month of my salary into the National Bank, into Mr. Holmes's account.'

'Next time you are passing, Inspector.'

'And to further demonstrate my gratitude, I shall drop a little something into that... that establishment you frequent in Kingly Street. I shall make it my highest priority upon my return to London.'

I thanked the Inspector. He donned his trilby and left the hotel. During this exchange Sherlock Holmes pretended to be busy elsewhere, tidying up the papers on the desk, such was the taboo of discussing money for our services. Now, he turned to face me.

'Watson! It is another triumph! We have saved an innocent man from the gallows and sent a multiple murderer to the hangman.'

'Indeed, Holmes, it has been another great success. This tale will write up admirably for Newnes. I shall make a start upon it in the morning. But first off, I think we should raise a glass or two to Mr. McCartney, Miss Turner and Inspector Lestrade. What do you say, Holmes?'

The great detective looked at his pocket watch. 'It is getting late. We should find some supper in Ross, during which you can enquire of the locals where we might find some more robust entertainment.'

I whistled. 'Humpin' bumpkin!' I declared, in my best Southern States drawl. And Holmes smiled, perhaps more at my enthusiasm than my impersonation but, just as we made the pact, the hotel receptionist appeared once again at the door. He was clutching a piece of paper.

'Telegram for you, Dr. Watson. It is from London and marked "urgent."'

It was from Mrs. Hudson. I ran my eyes over the text: "My dear John, we have an unexpected visitor. She is Elspeth Moriarty and she is Sherlock's nanny. Her health is failing as fast as I write this. I fear the worst. Come quickly."

I read this aloud to Sherlock Holmes. He sprang into action before I had finished.

'Hurry up, Watson! We can still catch the last train back to London, if we make haste!'

And that, dear reader, was the abrupt end to my first proper murder case outside of the metropolis. It was a satisfactory outcome, and I heard that it bore a happy and unexpected conclusion. Gerald Turner was put before the Assizes just a few days later, and the judge took pity upon his dreadful illness, and the lingering death that the Australian would have to endure and ordered the execution to be carried out that very afternoon. Good chap!

James McCartney was released and is now married to his beautiful, violet-eyed daughter. As far as I am aware, they live near Ross in complete peace and harmony.